TALES FROM I

GRANT WILSON

For Emma

CONTENTS

Author's Note

I would like to say that I have always wanted to be a writer. I'd like to but it wouldn't be true. Writing came later to me than most authors. But stories? Stories have always interested, intrigued and excited me. Horror stories in particular.

Horror covers such a wide range of emotions. It can exhilarate, terrify, disgust, astound and cut deep to the core (pardon the pun).

Horror can display complex metaphors in a visceral way that other genres just never could for me.

It can change your everyday life (how often do you still check the cupboard or over your shoulder in the mirror for monsters?).

It could come home with you after the cinema. It could lie next to you after you finish a chapter in bed. It can warp your very reality.

We as a species have evolved to be paranoid to survive. We have evolved as a race to be morbidly curious to thrive and prosper. Horror is at the heart of humanity and deep rooted in our brains. It unites us all. We are all scared of something after all. That is why I find it so brilliantly relatable and the perfect vessel for stories.

The three following stories did exactly that; took root in my brain and wouldn't leave me alone until I put pen to paper (or finger to key). They also deal with people struggling with their version of reality. I hope you enjoy them and are surviving with your own version of reality.

The Thin Man

The nurse smiles gently and gestures to the empty waiting room I'd been in ten minutes earlier.

'The doctor will be back with you in five minutes,' I'm told before she scurries off to carry on closing up.

It's late October and I am the last appointment of the day. I take a seat, opposite to the door, in the corner of the now dimly lit waiting room. It is dark outside and, with the lights out in the usually florescent lit hall, the black from outside seems to seep in through the pitch-black windows.

The doctor's office is an old converted manor house with whispers of former grandeur. Each room is high ceilinged with intricate wood work running around their edges but now it's been coated with sterile pastel gloss paint, covered in posters about health and wellbeing, and empty apart from cheap flat-packed chairs circled around the walls.

Fragments of the conversation with the doctor chase each other in my head but one sentence shouts above the rest; 'We can increase the dosage but if they keep getting worse, we may have to look at… other options.'

The last two words now ringing in my head. Doctors are meant to have your best interest at heart. They take an oath swearing to do everything they can to help but everything he has given me is just making me worse…

I'm lost in an angry swarm of thoughts when I hear the front door of the building open and close. After a few seconds of listening to shuffling footsteps approach, a man appears in the open entrance to the waiting room. The man is old and ancient looking. He is tall, six foot six at least, and is extremely thin. He seems to be wearing what at first glance looks like a suit but after closer inspection the jacket is too long at the back, like something a dinner guest might wear. Or an undertaker.

The skin stretched tight over his sallow cheeks looks grey and his sunken eyes find mine. He gives his head a jerky nod towards me and sits in the opposite corner next to the window.

I catch myself staring at the new addition to the room and quickly look away. I'm sure I was told that I was the last

3

appointment. The nurse is even locking up and half the lights are out. Maybe he doesn't know the surgery is closing for the night?

I glance at the man and to my dismay he's staring right back at me. I look away sharply, embarrassed a little to be caught looking.

He somehow looks familiar. Maybe I've seen him around? Hillwood is a small town after all, it is possible.

I look over at the man again, trying to pin point where I recognise him from, only to be met by his dark eyes once more. This time I don't look away so quickly. I hold his gaze and offer a friendly smile and nod. The old man's thin lips spread as his face contorts itself into a menacing, maniacal grin.

Horrified, I look away and try to distract myself with the posters around the walls. He's old and maybe just a bit senile. Maybe he doesn't have full control over his face and is just trying to be friendly back? I continue to concentrate on the walls.

'Learn to recognise a stroke!'

'Depression and you. What you need to know.'

'Lose weight in these 5 simple—'

Did he get closer? Out of the peripheral of my vision I can see the off-white shine of his teeth as he still bares them towards me but they look nearer to me now, somehow. I pretend to look at a poster next to him but focus hard on the man himself.

He is sitting a seat closer.

Or is he?

Could be my imagination or maybe I didn't see it right the first time. After all, I only had a quick glance. Maybe it's just because he's making me uncomfortable, *that smile*, and I'm just imagining things?

I study my knees and try to stay calm. He's just an old man. His body and limbs look like sticks or needles. I'm sure if it came to it, I could easily knock him down. Repeating this to myself I look out the window.

Bad decision.

It's so dark outside that the window is nothing more than a black mirror, reflecting the room back. The man's reflection is staring at me, unblinking and still smiling that stretched smile. My eyes snap to the man in the room and somehow, without moving, he's not looking at the window but still steadily staring at me.

That's not possible. I should have seen him turn his neck or he should somehow be in a slightly different position for having moved but he isn't. And this time – yes – this time he is definitely one seat closer than before.

My heart jumps in my chest as my stomach drops, both desperately trying to exit the room without me.

I turn to the open entrance, desperate for a sign of the doctor or nurse but no hero comes to my rescue. I turn back to the man in what must have been only two seconds later and again, he is one seat closer, his lips still split across his face and still sitting in the exact same position like some grotesque statue.

There are now only four seats between us and I'd have to run past him to get out the door. Panicking, I look around the room for a weapon or something to protect myself but there's nothing here but fucking chairs. My eyes flash past the man and he is still coming closer but somehow not moving.

Three chairs left.

'WHAT THE FUCK!' Escapes from me in a blast as the shock of his most recent move makes my body jerk in the seat. 'WHAT DO YOU WANT?'

The man doesn't move an inch or say a word. He just grins.

'Seriously, what the fuck?!'

I risk another glance at the door and when my eyes return the man is another seat closer.

Two seats left.

I rise out my seat on shaky legs and try to push myself and the chair as close to the wall as possible. Anything to get more space between me and this aged old man. I feel my palms slip against the arms of the chair with sweat. The hair on the back of my neck is on end, prickling me. Every inch of my being is screaming for me to run, to get out. That I'm in danger.

My eyes are still darting around the room frantically when he somehow is in the seat right next to me. I'm trapped in the corner like a fly by this spider legged man.

'Please,' I start to beg. 'Please don't.'

I blink and his face is inches from mine.

The empty grey eyes, the rows of yellowing teeth, the thin, cracked smile. All of it in my face. I can smell rotten meat and mud coming from him in powerful waves.

There is a pause where I don't dare to move. Where I can't. I stand comatose, unable to move, pressed against the wall. I've been caught.

And then all at once the man opens his mouth wide and lunges forward, arms now outstretched towards me.

I flinch, shutting my eyes instinctively and throwing my arms up to protect myself, my bodies last defence in the hopeless situation.

I fall back onto the chair.

There is silence apart from my harsh and shallow breathing. I open my eyes and the room is empty. Empty apart from the chairs lining the walls. No sign of any life apart from me. There is still the smell of mud in the air but much thinner now and weakening with every quick breath.

I slump over trying to catch my breath, staring around the room, trying my hardest not to blink in case I'm met with the face of the man again but when the inevitable happens I'm only met with the same extravagant and sterile room. The smell of mud and meat now completely gone, there's nothing to suggest anyone has been here apart from me.

'Ahhh Mr Wright...?'

I snap my head up and towards the entrance. My doctor walks in, gently smiling towards me but the smile falters a little when he sees my face. 'Everything ok?'

After a second, I nod and the smile is reinstated on the doctor's face.

'Good. Well I'm sorry to have kept you. Last appointment of the night and all. Just had some packing up and some sorting to do but here is your prescription.'

He hands me the pink slip of paper and I look down at it. Amongst the medical garble I'm able to make out my name, the surgery's address and the medication; Thorazine: Chlorpromazine – 200mg.

'Now as we discussed earlier, this won't cure you but it will help if you stick to the dosage.'

I stand up and pocket the pink slip of paper and mumble a thank you, still checking the room with my heart pounding in my chest. The doctors smile widens as he says, 'Ok, well I'll see you in a few weeks' time for a check-up, all right?'

'Yeah, see you then.' I say as I walk past him and towards the entrance. Just as I'm leaving the room, I look over my shoulder at the room one last time.

The doctor is stood in the middle of the waiting room watching me go but he is not alone. The old man is stood directly behind him, stooping so that only a sliver of his skeletal face is showing behind the doctors. As I watch, the thin man lifts his arm and waves goodbye and the doctor mimics the movement, as if the doctor was a life-sized marionette, tied to the thin man's body.

I turn and run towards the exit, flying past the bewildered nurse. 'Is everything—' She starts.

'Yes. I just– I'm late.' I manage to stutter out and with that I leave the surgery at a quick walk, not quite a run, out into the cold autumn night.

I walk aimlessly in the amber glow of the streetlights through empty streets. Every discoloured shadow reaching for me like the monster I left with the doctor.

I put my hands in my pockets against the cold and feel the prescription slip sitting there.

The pills.

I pull the slip from my pocket and stare at it for a long time, the angry swarm of thoughts deafeningly buzzing through my mind again. Should I get them? If that thing was controlling the doctor, can I even trust him? What if it's all the other pills he's given me that's started this? I know I recognised that man but where from?

I feel cold breath on the back of my neck and picture the thin man right behind me, working me like a puppet just like the doctor and I spin around. Nothing but sharp autumn wind greets me.

I pass a bin spot lit under a streetlight and I pause. The questions pound in my head. I make up my mind, crumple the paper up and toss it in the bin.

I don't know how long I stand there staring at the bin but my focus is broken when I see a man huddled against the cold coming towards me out of the black. Our eyes meet and he smiles a small polite smile. I smile back, a thin, cracked smile, as he passes.

'I'm fine,' I think to myself as I start to walk in the same direction. 'I'm just being paranoid.'

<u>St Julians</u>

The car pulled into the drive exactly parallel with the grass. Gracie Owens sat motionless behind the steering wheel, hands resting at precisely ten and two. The electric engine whirred to a still and the night was silent.

She drew a slow breath and tried to quiet the buzzing in her head. She hadn't felt herself that evening and thought a drive would help, they usually did, but they had begun to take longer to ease her condition.

Her eyes looked instinctively to the rear-view mirror and she saw the letterbox view of her own dark face looking back. Gracie was not an ugly woman but nor was she pretty. She had an average face that you could easily forget. She was average height, average weight and average in every other way.

She noticed a strand of hair had come loose from her severe ponytail. Her hands whipped up and she meticulously un-did and re-did the ponytail, ensuring every hair was in its place.

Putting her hands back to ten and two she noticed the time glowing from the dashboard and was reminded she was out of her routine. She could feel the unrest rising behind her eyes. The itching burn that came from not following the rules in her head. A late night was not unknown to her, and was sometimes necessary, but it did not stop her cheeks flushing as her obsessive-compulsive disorder bubbled up in her head, whispering to her that she should be in bed over and over.

She looked around making sure not to make too much noise for the neighbours, not that there was much point. Gracie lived at the end of a quiet lane next to a small wooded area. She had only one immediate neighbour, Mrs Baker, who was elderly and as deaf as a post. Mrs Baker liked Gracie as she was polite and sometimes did her shopping for her. Gracie liked Mrs Baker too however was always worried her late drives would disturb her aged neighbour but she had never mentioned it to her yet.

She slowly clicked open the door and got out the car, saw it wasn't parallel enough to her liking and got back in to correct it.

10

Everything timed out just as she liked; wake up at seven o'clock, morning pee and then shower at 7:35 a.m., out by 7:45 a.m., dry her hair and put it into the same ponytail she always did up to 7:55 a.m.

Just before eight she sat down to her porridge and put on the news.

'Good morning.' Greeted the smug newscaster, 'Here are today's headlines. Fears grow in Syria after a rebel attack on military forces, the Prime Minister is forced into making a statement on allegations of corruption within 10 Downing Street, and police are still appealing for information in relation to the murder of two people in the Greater Glasgow area.'

At 8:30 a.m. she was pulling out of the drive and was on her way to work. Gracie liked Hillwood, with its scenic views and privacy that the surrounding hills and wooded areas brought with it.

It wasn't too small and, with it closely neighbouring another four or five small towns and only a forty minute drive from the city, it was perfectly placed in her opinion.

The view had always reminded her of a turbulent sea. The hills rippling below with treetops and houses were rolling waves that gradually expanded to a calm sea of different coloured city lights in the distance. Hillwood was a tidal wave, looming over it all, threatening.

The only variations to the normal this morning were the increased police presence and another news van that drove past as she turned into the school.

Gracie taught Primary 6 at St. Julians Primary School. A good Catholic school where she had gone as a child, and not much had changed since then she thought as she walked into her classroom. The tables and chairs had always seemed bigger as a child but the coloured paper and drawings on the walls, the worn, hard carpet in the classroom and shiny linoleum of the halls (and even some of the staff) remained exactly the same.

She placed the bags of worksheets and jotters on the floor just as the bell rang. She met Mrs Carmichael, the other Primary 6 teacher, at the top of the stairs and together they went to let in the children.

Mrs Carmichael didn't much care for Gracie. All the other teachers loved her. She was polite, good at her job and they enjoyed her awkward and weird presence as 'quirky' but not Mrs Carmichael. She found Gracie to be too odd but couldn't quite put her finger on it. Gracie had never given her any reason to be disliked and had always been positively pleasant towards her but even still, Mrs Carmichael treated Gracie with the same cold, calculated way as you would a lying child.

They exchanged small talk as they got to the door and opened them to two lines of thirty excitable children. The small talk finished, thankfully Mrs Carmichael thought, and Gracie ordered her children up the stairs first.

'Hi Mum!' One of the girls in Gracie's line shouted at Mrs Carmichael as she passed.

'Hello Bethany.' Mrs Carmichael said back with a small smile. She caught eyes with Gracie who smiled at the pair and Mrs Carmichael turned away.

It took ten whole minutes for the class of ten and eleven year olds to take their bags off, put their plimsoles on and sit at their desks.

Gracie stood at the head of the class, growing slightly impatient. Just like her home life, her work life had to run on time.

'Good morning everyone,' She said.

'Good morning Miss Owens.' They chorused back in that sing song voice that only kids can seem to achieve in unison.

The morning consisted of maths problems and worksheets. She stood at the front of the class with the white board and explained the process for long division. She then set each group to work and prowled the room giving help to the children in the class that needed it. She had to tell Matt Burke and Barry McKechnie twice to stop talking, managing to keep the OCD from flaring, and sat for a full ten minutes with Natalie Mitchell who didn't grasp the concept, mainly because she didn't care.

Natalie was one of those students that the teachers talked about in the staffroom. She was only eleven and wore hair extensions, was covered in makeup and was constantly on her phone which was, of course, banned from school. She didn't try in class and as a result was the worst achiever in the school and most teachers had given up on her.

'If she doesn't want to learn then there's nothing we can do!' was the general consensus among the staff. Gracie, however, believed that Natalie was just a victim of her circumstances. Natalie didn't live in the nicest of areas in Hillwood and had a rough upbringing which had resulted in her now living part time with her grandmother. She could do the work, and was quite good at it, but only when she put in the effort.

This was in stark contrast to Bethany Carmichael who Gracie had sat next to Natalie in the hopes Bethany's high results and good work rate would rub off on her. Bethany was also talked about in the staffroom but the message changed depending if her mother was there. If Mrs Carmichael was present everyone would say how lovely she is and what a bright child she is. If Mrs Carmichael was absent from the chat however it would be more along the lines of 'what an annoying know-it-all.'

They continued to work until the bell signalling break went off. The kids threw their pencils down and ran to get their jackets and shoes on in a crescendo of laughing and shouted talk. Once the last of the children had left for the watery sun outside Gracie made her way to the staffroom for her regular cup of tea.

The staffroom was full of teachers refuelling after their first shift of broadening minds, with tea and light gossip. Chrissy waved Gracie over. Chrissy Easedale was the youngest teacher at St. Julians at just twenty-four and had taken a particular liking to Gracie, perhaps because they were closest in age or perhaps because Gracie had always been happy to help out Chrissy when she was stuck with what to do. Either way, Chrissy had made a habit of having Gracie's tea ready for her on her break and Gracie had appreciated the precise way Chrissy made it.

'How's your day going?' Chrissy asked holding out the cup.

'Well, and yours?' Gracie said as she accepted the cup and sat on the hard cushioned chair next to Chrissy.

'Yeah it's going good. Sam drew me a picture. Dunno what it is but he said it was me and he's just adorable so day made so far. You do much last night?' Chrissy gabbled. Gracie liked Chrissy but she did talk a lot and very quickly. Gracie was happier in silence.

'No, just did some marking and then TV. Yourself?'

'Well, I was meant to be going to the pub to meet with some friends for a couple of drinks and a catch up but after everything that's happened, I didn't really want to leave the house, you know?' She gave a knowing, ominous look to Gracie and continued at break neck speed, 'So me and Paul just sat and watched TV until the news came on and then *they* started talking about it and I thought sod this so we put on Netflix and had most of a bottle of wine between us.'

She paused for a sip of tea and then prattled on, 'I mean two already! I'm so glad I don't have kids yet or I'd be worried sick! I just hope they find the guy who's doing it soon and this all stops, touch wood.' She leant forward and lightly tapped the low wooden coffee table that the chairs surrounded.

Gracie continued to nod and took a sip of tea so as to let Chrissy carry on. She continued to speak rapidly about murders that had occurred with the same hushed but excited tones people use when talking about their neighbours but are terrified they might over hear.

Gracie looked around the room, nodding and repeating things like 'mm hm' and 'yeah' to satisfy Chrissy but she had become interested in the rest of the staff. There was a total of fourteen full time teachers at St Julians, one for every class and around four supply teachers to cover absences and holidays. The small square staffroom currently housed ten full time teachers and one supply who were all huddled in small groups either around the kettle on the counter at the back of the room or around the large coffee table in the middle. Usually the talk was loud and rabbling as one person from each group would bitch and moan about their class or the council or their husbands or boyfriends and rest would all listen and nod and agree that it was just terrible. Occasionally people from one group would hear the subject of another and shout across their feelings on the subject but today...

Today was very subdued from the normal. Gracie noticed worried faces and hushed discussions and it seemed that everyone was talking about the recent goings on in the town. Gracie zoned back in to catch the last of what Chrissy was saying, 'And I mean having all the extra police around should comfort us, right? But it just makes me more nervous, like, it just shows it's a big deal. What do you think?'

'Well... I can see what you mean; the increased police presence is troubling...' Gracie paused to drain her tea but before she could continue Charlotte had cut in from across the coffee table, 'Oh my god Chrissy did you see I'm a celeb last night?!' And Chrissy responded with a 'Oh my god!' before launching into speech.

Gracie relaxed back in her chair a little and watched the two women talk. She didn't like talking about the recent events, it made her nervous.

A little while later the bell rang and they had to once more collect the children. Mrs Carmichael and Gracie got the children in silence this time with just a brief smile for interaction.

'Hi Mum!' Bleated Bethany.

'Hi dear.' Mrs Carmichael said gently.

The second half of the morning went without incident. It was taken up by spelling tests and English exercise sheets. Gracie had to once again tell Matt and Barry to stop talking, cheeks starting to flush, but didn't have to sit with Natalie at all which was a rarity for her.

The time passed quickly and soon lunch was upon them. The bell rang and once again the children made a quick exit to the overcast Autumn day. Gracie grabbed her lunch and made her way to the staffroom once again.

She sat down next to Chrissy, who was already deep in conversation with Charlotte about I'm A Celeb again, and began to eat. About half way through the lunch break the staffroom door opened and James Craig, the headmaster, came in with an uncharacteristically grim face. He stood at the head of the room and the chat slowly quietened before dying.

'Thank you, ladies,' he said in his deep serious voice. He was a kind man who was nearing the end of middle age which was shown by his widow's peak hair line and his lined face.

'Now I know we have all been shocked by the recent events in Hillwood but I come with some unfortunate news,' There was a ripple of unease among the staff. 'The police have just announced the discovery of a third victim and this time–'

He paused to let the outburst of shocked gasps and anguished whispers die out. He continued, 'And this time they have announced that the victim is a child of primary school age.'

The room was silent. James tried to carry on but his voice seemed to be less strong than it did before.

'I realize that this is shocking news but I ask you all to be strong and vigilant. We are going to implement some new safety rules as of tomorrow which we will cover at an emergency assembly tomorrow morning. There will also now be a policeman stationed at the school in the mornings and afternoons to oversee the children at the start of school and at home time. If you see anything suspicious at all please let myself or Miranda know and we will alert the authorities.' He gestured to the hall door behind him which had Miranda Leaves' office on the opposite side.

Miranda was the Depute Head of St Julians and was largely useless, or so the majority of the faculty thought. There was a slight shifting in the room as everyone tried to imagine Miranda being able to do anything of worth, let alone helping with a serious issue like a murderer.

His voice regained its strength and he said, 'Everything will be covered tomorrow. Now obviously we don't want to mention this to the children yet and cause a great panic. We will hopefully have leaflets from the police to hand to the children that they can pass to their parents tomorrow. I'm trusting you all to be responsible and keep a closer eye on your children than normal.'

His voice softened for a second, 'And if you need any help or anytime to check in on anyone, we will try to accommodate.' And with a little nod to the room he turned and left, leaving a stunned silence behind.

The bell rang a short while later and the quiet that had stayed in the room seemed to break.

The excited screams and yells of the children packing up their games and lining up made the feeling inside the school all the more bizarre. How could they continue to play or be happy with what had happened?

Gracie and Mrs Carmichael collected the children once again in silence but no small smiles passed between them this time.

'Hi mu—' Bethany had started but faltered as she saw her mother's face. Mrs Carmichael had gone the pale shade of paper and did not answer. She instead stared solemnly at Bethany and allowed her to be swept up the stairs by the surge of children behind her.

The afternoon consisted of the year's project which, for Gracie's class, was the Victorians. A subject she enjoyed more than the children it had seemed for most of them had stopped the enthusiastic talk from lunch and now sat, eyes wide and unseeing while she talked to them about the Victorian way of life. She then set them the task of drawing what they thought Victorians would do to entertain themselves.

Within minutes the entire class were scribbling away in their jotters, all except Natalie. Gracie was sat at her desk surveying the class when she noticed the lack of movement from Natalie. The news from James was still playing in her mind, unsure of how to process it. She wasn't sure trying to persuade a horrible eleven-year-old to draw a Victorian child playing with a hoop and stick would do her mind any good but Natalie had leant back in her chair and was looking towards her pocket.

Why do kids think we can't tell what they're doing? Gracie thought. *I mean, I can clearly see your phone in your hands. You're the only one leaning back while everyone else is sitting forward working and you have previous for using it. Horrible wee brat, it's not hard to follow the rules.*

She sighed internally and stood up, making sure the seat scratched a little on the floor, giving Natalie a warning to hide her phone as Gracie wasn't in the mood for it, not today. Not with everything that had happened.

17

Natalie gave a slight jerk, saw Miss Owens walking slowly her way and slipped the phone back into her pocket.

'How are you getting on Natalie?' Gracie said gently.

'I don't get the point.' Natalie said bluntly.

'Oh?' Questioned Gracie. 'The point of what?'

'Of this exercise. How will this help us in high school?' Natalie demanded.

Gracie sat down in her usual spot opposite Natalie and looked her square in the face. Natalie's spot marked face stared cheekily back, not backing down. Bethany looked up from her drawing, sensing the incoming strop. A few of the other children had looked around too.

'Well you need it to show dedication. It can show you put in attention to detail and show other teachers how much time and effort you are willing to put into something. It also shows—'

Natalie cut across her, 'But that has nothing to do with the other subjects. This is pointless.'

Gracie took a deep breath and started again, 'It can also show how much of the subject and the lesson you have understood and how much you have retained and are able to recall.'

'But it's just a kid with a bloody hoop!' Natalie exclaimed.

'Do not use that language in my class, Natalie.' Gracie said and she could feel the anger beginning to bubble. She was losing her calm. This was the last thing she needed.

'Bloody isn't even a swear word though! And I'm not going to do the work. It's literally stupid.' Natalie cried and more of the class turned to see her meltdown.

'Natalie, I am not asking. I am telling you now, do your work. You understand it perfectly well.' Gracie growled through clenched teeth.

'No! It's actual pointless and won't help so why bother.'

'Natalie do your—'

Natalie cut her off again, 'I won't! You can't make me. It's just stupid.'

'Do not speak to me like—'

'I'll speak to you how I bloody wa—'

18

'NATALIE MITCHELL, YOU WILL DO AS I SAY OR YOU WON'T—'

'Miss...?' A small voice said and Gracie felt something small touch her hand. She withdrew it from the desk with a snap, horrified at being touched by one of them and looked at what one had done it. Her disgust must have clearly shown on her face as Bethany quickly withdrew her hand from where it had touched Gracie's on the desk and held it close to her chest, as if wounded.

Gracie sat back in her chair and regained control as she looked around the room. Small shocked faces looked up at her, even Natalie stared at her, mouth open in disbelief. They had never heard Miss Owens shout before and none of them ever wanted to again.

Gracie rubbed the patch where Bethany had touched her hand, as if burned, and looked back at Natalie.

'Continue with your work Natalie.' She said simply in her usual, soft voice and instead of arguing Natalie grabbed a pencil and began to hastily draw on the paper. Taking their cue from her, the rest of the class hurried back to work in silence in case they sparked more rage from their teacher.

Gracie quietly got up and walked slowly back to her desk. She paused and once satisfied that they were all working she slowly opened her bag and took out a small alcohol hand sanitiser and began to scrub her already raw hands. After several minutes of quiet scrubbing she could feel the burning itch begin to subside within her.

The bell rang at three o'clock and the children, still slightly subdued from the earlier outburst, left the room a little quieter and more orderly than usual. Gracie saw them to the bottom of the stairs and then returned back to her room. She sat at the desk and breathed. She didn't mean to shout at Natalie and no doubt her scummy mother would be on the phone later screaming how her child had been abused and how she'd go to the papers but Natalie had just got under her skin this time. Gracie looked at the pile of work on her desk. She could take it home with her but she never left work this early, bad day or not. She always left at exactly four forty-five and today was going to be no exception. She pulled the

19

mountain of sheets towards her and started sorting through and marking the papers.

It came to half past 3 when she decided she needed a drink of water. She got up and made her way to the drinking fountain at the other side of the open area from her classroom. She wiped the nozzle, *disgusting children,* and took a couple of sips of fresh, cold water. She leaned against the fountain and thought again of the news from earlier. It was terrible. *How could it have happened?* What would it mean for the school and the town?

She hated to see Hillwood like this. But just then, from behind her she heard the unmistakable creak of her classroom door. She spun around, startled by the noise but saw no one there. She walked briskly but cautiously to the door and pushed, letting it creak back open. She walked in and saw a sight to stop her heart.

'What are you doing? GET AWAY FROM THERE!' She yelled.

Bethany Carmichael had had her hand on the classroom cupboard handle and was in the process of opening it. She flinched when Gracie had started speaking and spun around, letting go of the now partially open door.

She let out a startled, 'Oh!' and Gracie moved forward grabbing Bethany by the arm and moving her away from the door.

'What are you doing?' She repeated forcefully.

'Miss Owens, I'm sorry I didn't mean—'

She began to splutter and tears started beading at the bottom of her eyes.

'Bethany, what were you doing with the cupboard?'

'I-I came in because mum is taking ages and I thought I co-could work on my drawing and—'

'Yes, and what about the cupboard?' Gracie cut across, getting impatient.

'I-I heard something move in the cu-cupboard and thought I'd see what it was.' Bethany finished, sniffing.

'I have told you and the class before Bethany, that no one goes into the cupboard. That is the teacher's area and could be dangerous to little girls. You could have been trapped if the door had locked behind you. It is not safe and you know not to go in.'

20

Gracie said before adding, more to herself than Bethany, 'Not even the cleaners go in there. No one but me goes in there.'

She looked at the child's blubbering face and softened her voice.

'Bethany, it's ok. I'm sorry if I frightened you but you know not to go into the cupboard. Like I said, it can be dangerous and I just have your safety in mind ok? Here.' She went to her desk and got out a tissue. 'Take this. I'll investigate the sound from the cupboard. You run along; you can carry on with the drawing tomorrow.'

She took the tissue with a shaky hand and wiped her face. She stammered a small 'sorry' before turning and leaving the room. Gracie followed her to the door and closed it behind her.

She turned and faced the cupboard. *Bethany had heard a noise, had she?*

Gracie walked forward to the door and swung it slowly open. The small cupboard was dimly lit by a single swinging bulb and had two large shelving units tightly packed with piles of old jotters, old wall decorations and spare trays for the children's desks. There was no one in there.

It was only after Gracie had confirmed the cupboard was devoid of people that she saw it. Looking down across the hard carpet that continued into the tiny room she saw a duffel bag had fallen over and its contents had spilled across the floor. Gracie looked in horror from the bag to the bloody knives, the blood-soaked clothes and, worst of all, a human hand lying limply on the floor, palm up. A gasp of surprise escaped her and she spun around. The room was totally deserted and the classroom door was tucked away in a corner meaning no one could peek in.

She turned back to the bag and stared towards it for a long moment, taking in the terrifying scene. The light shined off the knife, turning the light at the bottom of the cupboard a shade of bright red. The hand, small in size, lay like a dead spider, curled fingers pointing rigidly to the ceiling. Gracie could see the bone protruding from the stump where the hand had been severed.

She slowly leant towards the hand, taking in all its gruesome details; the finger prints, the scratches, the pale, bloodless colour. She reached out and grasped it. It was cold to the touch.

Stupid, she thought before tossing it back in the bag.

How could I be so stupid? I need to stop leaning the bag against the wall. Must have fallen over again and this, she picked up her blood-stained clothes from the night before and shoved them back into the bag, *This is what happens when you're stupid.*

She picked up the knife and looked at it, the light glinting in her eyes. Yes, her late night outing the previous evening had been cathartic but was now worrying.

The message from James. How had they found the child so soon?

She had thought it would have taken days to find the remains in the woods. And such a close call with Bethany.

Bethany, oh what she would give to take her tools to that disgusting little child and see the look on her mother's face when she heard the news. Especially after she touched her with her disgusting little hand. Or that monster Natalie.

How dare she speak to her like that? How dare she make her show her true face to the class. Disgusting and unclean, they needed to be cleaned.

To be clean.

The itching in her head flared as it had been doing more often recently. She longed for her hand sanitiser, seeing the mess had made her feel unclean. She clung to the thought that the reason she had not been caught yet was because she had rules and she stuck to the rules in her head, *oh yes*. The burning unrest kept her safe.

It couldn't be anyone that she knew. It would be too risky regardless of how much she wanted it.

She placed the knife in the dark bag and placed it behind the door, on the floor. It couldn't fall over this way. She may need to move it now after that incident with Bethany. Her mother would surely become more suspicious and the increased police wouldn't help. That can be planned later, she thought before closing the cupboard. She sat back at the desk and looked at the clock. It was only quarter to four. She still had an hour left to do work before

22

leaving. As long as she kept to her routine, no one would notice her. She could fade back into her average life and disappear until her next late night outing.

No one would think differently of her acting strangely or snapping in class today. She had received terrible news after all, they were all on edge and who could blame sweet, innocent Gracie Owens for being upset.

She had everyone's best interest at heart, after all.

Flight HL9 44

I was on board Highlines flight HL9 445 when it went down in the Scottish Highlands. I have learned the stories of all passengers on board since the incident and while I only tell you about a few of these, they represent the other hundred people that went down with the flight.

Part 1

The Smiths

Alicia was celebrating her seventh birthday. She came running downstairs that morning, still in her pyjamas, to see her parents stood grinning next to a sizeable pile of presents. She ran and briefly hugged each of them before attempting to start ripping the presents open but David held her back.

'Woah there.' He said, 'Hold your horses! We have something special for you first.'

Dawn brought out her phone and started filming while David repositioned their daughter to face them under a rolled up banner. With a theatrical flourish only fathers are capable of he unrolled the banner and told Alicia to read it aloud. She sounded out the words in her little voice; 'For your seventh birthday we are going to DISNEYLAND!'

You could hear David and Dawn chuckling in the video as their daughter screamed the last word and proceeded to run around the house crying, laughing and generally reacting how you would expect a seven-year-old to behave to such news.

They managed to wrangle their daughter for long enough to take her to the computer with the Highlines airline logo of a cartoon highland cow clearly visible on the screen. David sat Alicia on his lap and said, 'We're going to click the button together, okay?'

She beamed up at him and put her small hand on the back of his, letting him guide it until the cursor hovered 'Buy'.

He clicked and her little finger followed his, confirming their fate. David felt a great weight descend on him. He shivered, unsure why he felt so uneasy just as Alicia burst into tears.

'Aww Hun, what's wrong?' Dawn cooed as she snatched her from David's lap.

'I–I don't know!' Wailed Alicia.

'David?' Dawn asked but David sat staring at his hand still on the mouse.

'David.' She repeated a little sterner which seemed to snap him out of his reverie.

'Aww darlin',' he said, getting to his feet quickly at the look his wife gave him, 'Everything's okay. You're just emotional! Lots of exciting things going on. Why don't you open some presents?'

Alicia seemed to relax at her father's words and after being lowered to her feet she walked, a little dejectedly, to her pile of presents.

By midday, Alicia had forgotten about the feeling that had made her cry but David still felt a niggling that he couldn't shake. When pressed by his wife what was wrong, he was quick to answer that 'Everything is fine.'

This was Alicia's day; he didn't want anything to ruin it.

Dr. Charlotte Jackson M.D

Charlotte hated meetings and in her profession that's all she ever seemed to do. Sit around a table and listen to everyone talk and push bullshit around the room until lunch when they could then go eat a £30 meal and feel important. She loathed the masquerade of work that was done. She had worked hard to be where she was instead of being handed down the position like the men in the room and she was still treated like just a nurse.

'So what you're saying is that there's going to be another case of Ebola and a potential outbreak?' Chris, a thirty-something man in an expensive suit, asked from the other side of the glossy table.

Ian nodded from the head of the table. He was a small, balding man and was the eldest in the room by at least twenty years. He was the only one who didn't consider themselves a big deal, besides Charlotte.

'We need to send someone to London for damage control and to head the team. It'll involve a press junket; you'll have to prepare a statement and be there until I deem it ok to return. This is a high publicity case.'

The table rustled with excitement as everyone knew how great an opportunity this would be, plus all the hotshots loved a bit of TV time.

'I'm up fir it!' Barked Alexander in his heavy Scottish accent. He was a tiny man who seemed to make up for his size with his voice.

'They'll need subtitles for you, Zander! No chance! I'd be better; I went for the foot and mouth one.' Richard scoffed, a smarmy mummy's boy, Charlotte had always thought.

'Aye and look how well that turned out!' Alexander bellowed from down the table. The rabble in the room rose to a roar as everyone yelled how suited they were for the assignment with only Charlotte staying quiet. Her and Ian's eyes met and he rolled his in exasperation as if to say *this again*.

'Gentlemen!' He shouted in his wheezing voice, 'Gentlemen, I have already chosen the candidate.' The rabble died immediately as the men waited with baited breath to find who would win the bragging rights.

'I have chosen Charlotte to head this assignment. Does anyone have any objections?'

The room seemed to deflate as everyone sat back in their seats disappointed. There was a significant sniff from Alexander and a mumbled, 'No, not at all' from Richard but the bitterness could be felt in the air.

'That's settled then. Charlotte,' he said, turning to face her, 'I'll need you to head down tomorrow, this is urgent and I want a good head start with it.'

'Of course.' She said, giving a slight nod.

'Ok.' Ian said, turning to his left. 'Next on the list is monthly stats. Bryan the floor is yours...'

The meeting lasted another two hours. It would have only been forty-five minutes if the men hadn't kept trying to one up each other or impress one another. She walked quickly through the corridors of the newly built hospital to her office; a decent sized room with a window for a wall looking down to the courtyard. She sat at the glass desk and paused for a moment to catch her breath.

She liked Ian and knew he had always appreciated the work that she had done. She made a mental note to fire him a quick email saying thanks as she booted up the computer and started making a list of things she would need. Half way through the list for the following day she realised she'd forgotten to book the flight down.

Damn! They'd better not be sold out. Alexander would never let me hear the end of it if I screw up on my first outing.

Her fingers flew over the keyboard searching for 'cheap flights to London'.

The first link brought up a page with a cartoon highland cow piloting a miniature plane. Charlotte sighed but clicked through the website regardless and finally found herself a seat.

As she clicked the pulsing 'Buy' button she felt a great chill rush up her arm and spread like icy water through her body. With a rasping gasp she jumped up and knocked the chair over in the process. She rushed to the window and looked at her faint reflection which looked back at her with anguish.

She took her pulse, which was racing, and her temperature, which was normal, but she still felt clammy.

Must just be the stress of all this hitting me at once, she thought, self-diagnosing. *I just need to calm down and get a grip.*

After a few deep breaths she could feel her heartbeat returning to its usual rhythm. She picked up the chair from the floor and continued planning her trip without giving her stress induced incident a second thought.

Robert Hall

'I promise you Dad, this time I'll make sure everything is worked out.'

It was a promise Robert had heard from his son one too many times to actually get his hopes up. He'd made similar promises before that he would visit or that he'd bring the grandkids to stay for a while but something always came up at the last minute or there was some reason they couldn't book anything or an error here and cancellation there.

'We've sorted the money for your flights. I'll wire it to you and all you have to do is book them yourself. I'd book it for you but I don't have all your details. You'll be all right booking it yourself?' Chris asked.

'I'll be fine... Fine. I know how to work it,' Robert said waving the comment away to his empty flat, 'but I can't take your money, son. I've got some I could—'

'Don't be daft, Dad. I'm sending it as we speak and besides, I owe you for the last time. Like I said; I'm making sure everything is sorted! So you'll need to sort the flights pretty sharpish. Just text me with the time of the flights and I'll get you from the airport.'

'Mmm...' Robert mumbled hesitantly. 'All right then. I'll send you an e-message or whatever with the details.'

Chris chuckled down the phone, 'An email Dad but yeah that'd be great. So I'll speak to you then. I love you Dad.'

'Ok, speak then. Love you too son.' Robert said just as the line disconnected. He sighed to himself as he hung the phone back on the cradle.

Maybe the boy will actually come through this time? Would be the first time in a long time. He's always been self-absorbed. Even when Joan died, he almost had to be convinced to come back home for the funeral. Never understood that I needed him even when he had no use for me.

Deciding to see if Chris had stuck to his word he slowly shuffled over to the computer and loaded it up.

He hated using the desktop computer. He had been a telecommunications engineer for the majority of his life, working with his hands, and while technology had been ever present in his life, he tended to steer clear and stick to what he knew.

Ten minutes and a cup of tea later he was on his online banking account (managing to get there by following the step by step guide the young man in the branch had written for him) and, sure enough, there was an incoming payment from Christopher Hall. He sat staring at it for a while, reflecting on the proof that his son may have actually come through for him this time.

He decided that he wouldn't get his hopes up until he saw Chris in the flesh and supposed he should sort out a means to get there.

Bringing up 'The Google' as Frank down the hall had shown him, Robert typed slowly and with a singular index finger 'one flight from Inverness to London please.'

Clicking the first link brought up a familiar looking cartoon cow that he was sure he had seen advertised at a bus stop in the city centre. Almost sure of it he proceeded slowly through the website, making sure that he was following all the instructions and double checking everything. Finally coming to the checkout, he clicked 'Buy'.

He felt a great sadness wash over him suddenly, making the air catch in his throat. He spluttered and doubled over in his chair trying to catch his breath. After a few deep, heaving gasps he managed to sit back and relax.

Must just be emotional. The thought of seeing Chris and of Joan popping into my head like that can catch me off guard.

He gathered himself together, decided to send the message to Chris about the flights later and thought, *at least I get to turn this bloody thing off* as he stabbed at the desktop's power button.

Graham and Leslie Rutherglen
'You make no effort at all!'

The words still rang around Graham's head from the last falling out as he sat in the study with his nightly can of cider (Or 'Crutch' as she called it).

How could she possibly think that I make no effort?! He thought. *After all I've done for her! I gave up the opportunity to work in the states, bought this ludicrous house (and her car), even moved to the middle of pissing nowhere because she was "sick of the city".*

He leant forward and nestled his can amongst the paperwork strewn across the glass desk.

Stupid bloody desk. Stupid bloody room! She couldn't even give me one room of the house to have as my own without her messing with it. I make no effort, hah! All I do is work and work and WORK while she tries her hand at whatever her "life's calling" is that month. Having to fund her being a florist or an interior designer or a beautician or making handmade jewellery.

He picked up another can, pulled the tab with a satisfying hiss and leaned back into the leather desk chair with a sigh.

He thought of Leslie and the argument from earlier that day. She had gone on to her latest folly of designer cakes which had started him off.

Sat in the kitchen that morning Leslie had announced to the room that she would proudly be going into business as a cake designer.

'And I just need £2000 for start-up and the proper equipment.' She had paused, looking at him expectantly.

'Where has this come from? I thought cake was bad for you? Doesn't that make your gym membership pointless?' He'd meant it to sound jokey but the bitterness had slipped through.

'I knew you would do this!' She started, 'You never take me seriously. I've got it all planned out and found a great set up from YouTube but no, you can't let me have this. You are stopping me from my true potential...'

She had carried on in this vein for another five minutes but Graham had heard it all before and by this point almost knew it off by heart.

He loved Leslie and of course wanted to see her prosper and be happy and the first few times she had given him this rant he had crumpled and given her exactly what she wanted but now he knew better. Now he knew that she knew the buzz words that would make him feel sorry enough to throw money at her. That was until she broke the usual ramble with; 'You make no effort at all!'

'I what?'

'You don't! You make no effort around the house or to better yourself or with us!'

There was a loud silence after these words where only the fridge was brave enough to make noise.

'I need to go to work.' He had said and he got up and left. They hadn't spoken since.

He looked at the can in his hand and to the papers everywhere on the desk. Maybe he wasn't bettering himself. He did drink too much and maybe he didn't help enough around the house but they had gardeners who did the garden and someone came to clean the house twice a week that *he* paid for.

She was right about the last one though, he didn't make an effort for them. Not anymore. He had put more time and effort into work and making sure she was taken care of than how she felt.

They used to go on city breaks all the time and she loved them.

He sat forward and cleared away the work covering the desk and pulled out his laptop. Memories flooded his head as he pictured past trips. He loved European cities, especially Paris. Being able to reach the heights of the Eiffel Tower and the depths of the Catacombs always felt like a full adventure and he knew Leslie loved the shopping experience. *Of course.*

He searched for city breaks and opened the first link to cheap flights to Paris.

He navigated through the Highlines website knowing Leslie would moan about flying economy seats and that they had one stop off in London but he didn't make his money by making frivolous purchases, she did plenty of that for him. He chuckled quietly to himself.

He raised the can to his lips and drank as he clicked the 'Buy' button and a chill ran through his body causing him to choke and slop a load of cider down his front. He spluttered and coughed, cursing all the while. Slowly regaining his breath, he put the can down and stood up to look down at his soaked front. He sighed deeply once again and thought, *Maybe I should stop drinking so much.* He shut the laptop over and headed to bed. He'd tell Leslie about the trip in the morning.

Sahir Saeed

The front door rattled sending a spasm of fear up his back.
Knock knock knock.

He picked his way through the dim, litter strewn flat and hesitantly pulled back the curtain on the front door. The blurred outline of a man was visible through the frosted glass. He opened the door slowly to reveal a man he didn't know holding a package.

'Yes?' He asked, trying to sound as normal as possible.

'Delivery for you.' Said the man. Sahir caught his eye and the man gave him a significant look and Sahir understood. His heart fluttered and his hands shook as he took the box from the delivery man. It wasn't too heavy but his arms strained at the weight. He set it down quickly.

'Thank you.' He mumbled and went to shut the door.

The man quickly held out a tablet, 'You must sign for this.'

'Oh—sorry.'

Sahir fumbled with the tablet and could see the man internally sighing. He gave it out for the man to take back and as the man leaned in, he gave a whisper that sounded more like a breath, 'Praise be, Brother.'

Straightening, he gave a little nod and left. Sahir quickly shut the door and locked it again. He knew the flat was being watched from time to time so he had to be very careful. He had been given strict orders to be careful but every sign from the outside world added a little more pressure to the already enormous weight on his shoulders.

He sat down and, after checking that the curtains were securely closed, he opened the package. He picked the note up first and read; "Brother. The time has come. Everything is in place. You know what you must do."

He set the note aside and gently lifted the contents of the box out and placed it on the table. The Semtex was housed in a polystyrene case which easily came apart to reveal the packed bag the explosive resembled.

It looks like something you buy at a butchers, he thought as he looked at the sausage shaped bomb. This absurdly shaped thing was the centrepiece for the plan, nearly everything revolved around it, and now him too.

He didn't know how long he had sat staring but the sound of a car accelerating outside snapped him out of his trance. The note was right; he knew what he had to do. Months and months of meticulous planning had led to this point. He knew he was on the bottom rung of the ladder and only knew what he was permitted to know but he was smart enough to understand the planning that was involved. The months of secret notes passed to him, the brief meetings with people he didn't know in places he didn't expect. He knew there was an entire invisible network around him that could see the master plan in action but he was just a soldier following instructions on a need to know basis.

The thought that he was just a gear in a large machine excited and terrified him.

He took a plate from the kitchen and set fire to the note on it. He had to leave no evidence of anyone else's involvement. They had been clear on that.

He then carefully moved the explosive to the loose floorboard under the rug, making sure it looked untouched and unassuming after he was done.

This arrival was the last signal he would receive from them and he knew the plan was nearing completion. He brushed the dirty plates and crisp packets off of the laptop sat on the coffee table and booted it up. They had carefully selected what airline to use, what flight, what time, what destination to cause the biggest message to the world. A message that would be strong and clear as a message from God should be. He would be a martyr, he thought. A beacon of righteousness for his brothers and sisters to follow. While he may not be the mastermind behind the message, he would be the face, the name, the legend that would be praised the world over by like-minded believers. There would be people who think him a terrorist, yes. But what made him different from the man in America that shot up abortion clinics? Or the man who opened fire in a gay club? Did they not do this in the name of their God? The only difference was the colour of his skin and the God in question.

The difference was that he was righteous and he would be greeted in heaven by God and welcomed as a hero.

He navigated the cursor around the Highlines website looking for the morning flight to London. He entered the details given to him on one of his meetings, a false identity and a fake card. He clicked 'Buy' and spasm of fear gripped his back worse than before. He jumped to his feet, toppling the table and shattering

34

plates across the floor. He ran to the only window that was next to the door and peered out behind the dirty curtain. There was no one there and no suspicious cars parked out front. He was still safe. He had to stay calm if the plan was to succeed and the plan *would* succeed, there was no alternative. It was God's will.

He forced himself to take a few deep and shaky breaths and could feel his heart rate start to settle back to normality. He must carefully pack now and prepare himself for what must be done.

Part 2

The Airport

1

Inverness airport always felt like it was pretending to be an airport to David and the same thought occurred to him now as it did every time he saw it from the outside; it's just a repurposed hanger. The routine was the same as other airports in Scotland; check in, go through security, wait at a gate for your flight then finally leave but he felt there were reminders that it was trying to be something it wasn't everywhere. For example, every time you looked up you could see the corrugated steel of the hanger roof or else it was the stall-like shops that, to David, looked like oversized plastic play shops that Alicia had.

He turned in the taxis passenger seat as they approached 'the hanger' and felt a rekindling of joy for the place as he saw the way his daughter was looking at it. Alicia was sat wide eyed and open mouthed at the building, eyes sparkling with adventure. She looked from the building to Dawn then to David and, realising he was looking at her, she said, 'Do they keep the planes in there?! How do they fit?'

David laughed, 'No honey, the planes are kept somewhere else out back.'

He caught Dawns eye and they both shared a smile. Alicia had been asking questions non-stop since she had woken up and didn't seem about to stop anytime soon.

'But I still don't get how the planes stay up?' She turned to her mum.

'Well, they float. Like a boat.' Dawn said smiling at her daughter's face.

'So—So they're like a balloon then?'

'Well no, not exactly. It's to do with the friction in the wings.' Dawn said hesitantly.

'Oh. I see.' Alicia said knowledgeably.

Dawn looked to David for confirmation, 'That's right isn't it?'

'Eh...' But before he could answer the taxi had stopped in the drop off point.

36

'All right folks, that's us here.' The taxi driver declared in his crisp Inverness accent and he jumped out the car to grab the bags.

'Here we go, you ready?' Dawn asked.

'Yeah!' Alicia cried, almost visibly shaking with excitement.

They grabbed their cases (over packed sturdy M&S ones for Dawn and him, and a small pink one for Alicia), paid the taxi man who bid them 'Bon voyage!', wheeled their way into the terminal and joined the queue.

2

Charlotte had all the patience in the world for most things, it was a necessity for the job, but there were certain things that managed to get under her skin. Namely people who were too slow. Slow walkers, slow drivers and people who held up queues by being too slow. The latter was now testing just how far her patience would go.

An old bugger was now fifteen minutes into conversation with one of the only two open check-in kiosks and the other desk wasn't going to win any records for service speed.

She took a deep breath and tried to stop herself from seething. Maybe this was just the stress of the situation finally catching up on her but she couldn't let Ian down. He had chosen her for a reason and she was determined to stay professional throughout. Even if it was just so she could rub it in those other idiots' faces.

A small, young family joined the queue behind her. She turned and her eyes met a young girl's.

'Hello!' The girl blurted out.

'Hello,' Charlotte replied with a smile.

'I'm going to Disneyland!'

Charlotte's gave a false but good natured inhale of shocked breath.

'Are you? That's wonderful. You're a very lucky girl.' She looked to the mother and father and smiled and had begun to turn to check if the queue had moved when—

'Are you going to Disneyland too?'

Charlotte faced the girl again, 'No, I'm going to London. To work.'

She leant towards the girl and whispered, 'Between you and me, it's really boring.' And she blew a raspberry. The girl exploded with giggles.

'Ok Alicia. Stop annoying the lady now,' said the father and he swept the little girl into his arms.

'Oh, not at all,' smiled Charlotte but she turned to face the line again. The old man was finally moving towards the security checks and the line was progressing again.

3

Robert didn't like modern airports. They relied too much on computers and were taking all the human elements out. It wouldn't be long before the nice lady he spoke to at check-in would just be a face on a screen and you'd be stuck on a conveyor belt and just wheeled through like your luggage.

He didn't care if he was a clichéd old man, he preferred to trust things where you could see where they kept their brain.

He reached security; another mess of technology he thought.

He'd stood in the queue for five minutes when the couple in front turned to face him.

'Excuse me,' The man said. He was middle aged and had a clear look of wealth about him. It was the pink polo shirt, Robert thought.

'Sorry but I think your phone is ringing.'

'My phone?' Robert checked his pockets and brought out the thick phone and as he did so the high pitched beeping that he had thought was one of their machines got louder.

'Bloody thing,' he muttered to himself. He gave an apologetic nod to the couple and, after another few seconds spent trying to remember what button it was, he answered.

'Hello?' He yelled.

'Dad? It's me,' Chris said, 'and you don't need to shout! I think we can hear you from all the way down here!'

There was the delicate sound of giggling girls after this.

'Are you with the girls then?' Robert said in a quiet shout.

'Yes, they're here. Say hello to Grandpa, girls.'

'Hi Grandpa!' They shouted in unison.

'When are you coming?' asked Julie. Or was it Abigail? He couldn't tell these days.

'Oh, I'll be there soon. I'm at the airport right now. You'll need to carry me when I'm there because I'll be so tired from flapping my arms flying down to see you.'

The girls squealed with glee at the vision of their feathered grandfather furiously flapping through the air.

'So, you're all right?' Chris' voice was back.

'Yeah son I'm fine. I'll see you when I get there.'

'Ok, we'll be waiting for you in arrivals. Safe flight, Dad. Love you.'

'Ok, I'll see you. Love you too.'

If I can find my way to arrivals. These places are mazes, he grumbled internally.

The line progressed slowly but surely with nothing out of the ordinary until—

BEEP

Robert looked over and saw a coloured man being pulled aside after setting off the metal detector. He watched as the security man started to talk to the man. The coloured man emptied his pockets and Robert saw with difficulty, he was sixty-five and his eyesight wasn't as good as it used to be, the man pull out a phone that looked just like the one he had. *Funny,* he thought, *one person who doesn't have one of those stupid iPhones.*

The security man nodded, took the phone from the man and put it back through the x-ray machine. Robert watched the coloured man. He couldn't put his finger on it but he thought there was something wrong. The man almost looked in pain but before he could squint and get a better look his phone had been returned to him and he had gone through to duty free.

4

Leslie snatched the belt from Graham's hand and hastily pushed it back through the loops on her jeans.

'Fucking joke.' Graham heard her mutter. She grabbed her jacket from the tray and without putting it away she threw a final dirty look at the old man who was in the process of setting off the metal detector again.

Graham knew better than to say anything. Leslie had taken a dislike to the old man after his phone had went off for too long and there was no rationalizing this sort of crazy, pointless hatred so he kept his comments to himself. After all, he didn't want to start this trip with a trivial argument when it was meant to be a chance to be closer to each other, so he smiled his best and followed on as she stalked through the duty free.

Keeping close behind, he followed her as she marched to the gate. She had moaned about the lack of shops at the airport from the second they had left the house and Graham had had to listen to the taxi driver agree and talk about a £1 million revamp planned.

'It's about bloody time!' She had said, 'I'm always disappointed how little is there. I always walk through and there's nothing worth getting! Just endless cuddly Nessie dolls. They won't get any of my money until they sort themselves out!'

Her money being my money, Graham thought with an inward laugh. She had been happily surprised when he showed her the plane tickets and he had even managed to hold back the argument when she moaned about not going on a 1st class flight. They had made up but it was still tense and a little forced but that would change once they got there and relaxed a bit.

Or at least he hoped it would. Her current mood said otherwise but he wouldn't give her a chance to complain about him. He took comfort with the thought of him doing something nice and half jogged as they got to the gate.

She sat, crossed her legs fussily and pulled out her jewel-encased phone (another failed business venture of hers).

5

Sahir watched as the seats at the gate slowly filled around him. A grumpy woman with a tired man sat opposite him and he watched as they sat in silence on their phones. Everyone around him was bent necked and staring at their own screens.

He alone was sat upright. He alone was righteous. He alone knew this world and what must be done.

40

What must be done...

He fought the temptation to check his pockets again. He didn't want to draw attention to himself by looking suspicious and he had already almost blown it going through the metal detector with his phone on him.

His heart had leapt to his throat and his spine had given the horrible and too familiar spasm of fear. The guard had asked for him to empty his pockets and he thought he had failed.

He was a disgrace.

He had failed God.

His mind had only stopped racing when the man had handed his phone back to him and given him a small, knowing nod. Only Sahir had seen this and he knew; this man was another cog in the machine. Another agent to protect him as he carried out what must be done.

What had to be done.

He had sat, barely moving for thirty minutes when the call came over the tinny speakers; 'Now boarding Highlines flight HL9 445 Inverness to London.'

There was a scramble as everyone rushed to get into the queue that was quickly forming in front of the desk. Sahir stood and walked through the crowd, not really seeing them, but walking through them as one might walk through dense forest in the dark; slowly, careful not to touch for fear of getting scratched.

He did not seem to be there in his own body. He watched as a passenger to his surroundings and allowed himself to be moved with the flow of the queue.

There were no questions at the desk as he knew there wouldn't be and felt his legs carry him out into the cold, the sun now slowly rising, casting long shadows and staining the sky a bright pink. Before he knew it, he was on the plane and being pointed to his seat. He sat surrounded in his euphoria and allowed the plane to fill. His mind quiet apart from one repeating message. Over and over.

What must be done.

What needs to be done.

What must be done.

41

Must be done.

PART 3

The engines roared and the plane rumbled as it picked up speed. The pilot pulled firmly back and everyone was pushed back into their seats as gravity tried to claim them from the air and the rumbling stopped. Within five minutes everyone was looking out the windows. The pink clouds more fully formed than the wisps they had been on the ground made the plane jostle. The small rural towns surrounding Inverness quickly shrank and were swallowed by vast forest, large fields and growing mountains.

A little girl could be heard whining about her ears being sore to be answered, 'Take a sweetie, it will help'.

The plane quickly levelled out and the ding for the cabin crew sounded through the plane. Immediately a blotchily tanned man began to walk effortlessly uphill along the aisle. The plane rolled in a turn and everyone sank back into their seats but this didn't stop the orange man walking from row to row asking people for 'Tea? Any tea or coffee here?'

They steadily rose and the patches of green below the plane disappeared behind the clouds that were growing thicker and thicker. The light in the cabin would dim and grow again as the plane powered through until finally bursting into the bright light of uninterrupted sun you only achieve above the clouds.

Twenty five minutes had passed of surprisingly smooth sailing through the sky. Charlotte had been rifling through papers and folders she had brought on with her but set them down and rubbed her eyes. She had been so absorbed in her work that she had neglected to notice how long of the flight had passed and how tight her eyes were getting. She leant back and took in her surroundings. From the back of the plane she could see the tops of everyone's heads in front, all chatting happily or, like the old man to her right, looking out the window at the clouds moving below them. The only person not moving was sat to her left.

He hasn't moved at all, she thought.

Sahir gave a deep sigh in his seat. He wiped the beads of sweat from his forehead with a shaking hand. He knew the time was coming.

'Are you okay?' Asked Charlotte turning to face him in her seat.

'Yes. Everything—Everything is in God's hands.'

Another ding passed through the plane as the seatbelt sign flicked off and it was answered with the clacks of dozens of belts clicking.

'What?' She asked the man. He looked pale, unwell.

'What did you say?' She had heard but did not understand. He turned and faced her. Their eyes connected and in them she could see; it was time. In that second, Charlotte understood.

'Please,' she whispered, 'Don't.'

He made a grab for his pocket but she caught his arm. She didn't know for sure what he was going to do but she knew from his face what he wanted.

She had seen the look in patients before. As an ambitious medical graduate, she had been shadowing Dr Nichol when a 'disturbed' patient who had been awaiting transfer to a secure hospital had strangled a nurse on her rounds. Charlotte and Dr Nichols had found the nurse blue faced with the patient above her. His and Sahir's eyes identical in intent.

'NO!' The shout rose in her throat as panic set in. They began to struggle side by side in their seats, him scrabbling for his pocket and her desperately trying to stop him. People were starting to turn in their own seats to see what the commotion and shouting was at the back of the plane. Two of the cabin crew, the blotchy orange man and a severe looking middle-aged woman started storming down the aisle, drawing more attention to the grappling couple at the back.

Robert, at the window seat on Charlotte's other side, watched on helplessly as Sahir managed to edge his hand into his pocket and bring out his phone.

Sahir pushed himself as far into the aisle as his seat belt would allow, breaking free of Charlotte's grasp. The cabin crew were almost upon him. He screamed a long primal yell that came more from his soul than his throat as he pressed the one and only number on speed dial.

44

Everything happened very quickly, almost at once. There was an almighty BOOM followed by metal screeching as a hole was ripped into the side of the plane. The force of the blast from the luggage hold spread and opened the cabin along one side like a tin can. The air from the speeding plane was sucked out, everyone with their seat belt on was thrown around in their chair. Everyone without their seat belt on wasn't so lucky.

Sahir watched through the blinding light of the sun now piercing into the plane as the two crew members, who had been mere inches away, were sucked out of the hole into the open sky.

The plane had opened where the little girl who had complained of sore ears had been sat. She had been sat in the middle seat flanked by her parents. Her seat and the man's seat were no longer there, just gnarled and bent metal.

The man and woman who had sat opposite Sahir in the departure lounge were in the seats directly behind the small family. The man wasn't moving and the woman was frantically trying to attach her oxygen mask to his face as soon as they flopped from the ceiling above the struggling passengers. His had been sucked out the hole along with so many others.

The plane lurched forward and everything not held down lifted into the air.

For a split second everything hung suspended in the air as if the crippled plane had broken through to outer space. The effect ended as the nose of the plane aimed for the ground below and gravity forced everyone again deep into their seats, hungry to reclaim them. The roar of the wind was deafening as the plane picked up speed.

Debris and luggage flew to the back of the stricken vehicle as it plummeted out of the sky. The sun looked like it was rolling around the cabin as the plane spun and spun in the nose dive they were caught in.

Sahir sat in his seat watching all of this happen in the space of seconds. He watched as a bit of metal spun past him and sank into the seats to his right. He didn't have to look but knew the woman and man were gone.

45

He thought he could hear screams but it could have been in his own head. The unquenchable voice of survival everyone has inside screaming for self-preservation.

He pulled the oxygen mask out of the way; he knew it would do no good now. He had achieved what he must do. He knew he would be greeted by God in heaven as a hero. His handler had told him so. *Promised* him.

Sahir looked along the aisle and his deepening calm was broken. The sun rolled up and away and up again as the spin got faster but there was a constant shadow at the head of the aisle. It didn't move with the wind stripping the insides into the sky and didn't vanish with the blinding sun, it just... was.

The sun darkened as the dive reached the thick clouds. Sahir now fought to keep his eyes open through the moisture whipping and stinging his face. This shadow could not exist but it did. And it started to move down the plane at a steady pace towards him.

It had no features but he knew it was somehow looking at him. It seemed to be walking but that would be impossible.

The shadow reached him just as the plane broke out under the clouds. He didn't and couldn't move as it seemed to lean towards him. They had seconds before the plane met the rolling green hill speeding towards them.

The roar of the plane seemed to fade and over the dimming noise Sahir heard the shadow, heard *me*, quietly whisper, 'There is no God. There is only darkness.' As the shadow swallowed him.

Epilogue

Bryan Watts

'It is believed that at this point Sahir Saeed set the device off remotely, crippling the plane and sending all passengers hurtling into farmland in the Hillwood area just outside Glasgow, but how did he get this far? Why did he do it? Did officials and law enforcement know of him and do nothing?'

The Webflix documentary cut from a CGI image of a plane nose diving into a field to an official-looking bespectacled man talking to someone just off camera. The tag on screen read 'John Armstrong - crash investigator, author of 'Horror in the Highlands - Flight HL9 445'.'

'It's speculated that the counter terrorist branches of law enforcement across Britain *were* aware of Sahir Saeed and many of the key players in this attack yet they failed to act in time. As I state in my book, the blame is just as equally on them for this atrocity.'

The six-part docuseries cut again to the same shots it had lured viewers in with; shots of the wreckage strewn across the field, a row of burnt out seats alone by a half-demolished house and a girl's pink suitcase.

Bryan stopped the episode. He hated stuff like this. All these docuseries were the same, showing you the same five clips of horrible devastation that would fill our morbid curiosity and keep people watching.

He switched tabs to check the chat he had open with his mates.

Ryan: Sorted! My dad says the cabin is free from the 19th till the end of the month! Only problem is he's got the car for business. Looks like UberBus for us :(

Adam: sack that. am no spending 5 hrs wi ma knees round ma ears.

John: :P

Greg: Train?

They all agreed and Ryan posted a link to Rail-Away, a discount site for train tickets. Bryan specified the agreed time and date into the cartoonish passenger car on the site, cringing at the ridiculous layout.

A long weekend away with the guys was going to be great, he'd been looking forward to it since Ryan had suggested it on the chat a week ago. He tapped his card details in by muscle memory and clicked 'Pay'.

A shock of cold shot up his arm and spread through his body like poison. The laptop fell off his lap and onto the bed as he half fell, half leapt out it.

He stood panting in his room as the cold slowly began to fade. He passed it off as excitement mixed with his second can of energy juice of the evening.

'I need to stop drinking these.' He said to the room at large as the cold fully left him and he got back in to bed.

I was on board the 9:45 a.m. Scot-Way service from Glasgow to Arntocher when it derailed off the Stornbridge Viaduct.

All Characters in this book are fictitious, and any resemblance to actual persons, living or dead (living impaired), is purely coincidental.

Printed in Great Britain
by Amazon